WONDERWORKS

DONNING

Virginia Beach/Virginia

WONDERWORKS

Science Fiction and Fantasy Art
by
Michael Whelan

Edited by Polly and Kelly Freas

A STARBLAZE SPECIAL

FOR AUDREY

Library of Congress Cataloging in Publication Data

Whelan, Michael, 1950-
  Wonderworks: science fiction and fantasy art.

  (Starblaze editions)
  1. Whelan, Michael, 1950- 2. Science fiction—
Illustrations. 3. Fantasy in art. I. Freas, Polly.
II. Freas, Kelly. III. Title.
NC975.5.W48A4 1979   741.9'73   79-12575
ISBN 0-915442-75-2 library
ISBN 0-915442-74-4 paperback
ISBN 0-915442-83-3 limited

Large, art quality prints of some of the pictures in this book are planned. For information write: Michael R. Whelan, 172 Candlewood Lake Road, Brookfield, Connecticut 06804.

With Contributions by:
POUL ANDERSON
C. J. CHERRYH
ALAN DEAN FOSTER
ANNE MCCAFFREY
MICHAEL MOORCOCK
GERALD W. PAGE
And Comments by the Artist

CONTENTS

The dignity of the artist lies in his duty of keeping awake the sense of wonder in the world.

— G. K. Chesterton

EDITOR'S NOTE:

Perhaps more than any other genre, fantasy has always been a highly visual medium, attracting artists and publishers of every taste and calibre, all eager to produce beautiful books. The case for science fiction has been somewhat different.

For instance, almost never have there been as many as a dozen top-flight artists working the field at the same time—largely because the genre is extremely demanding, and the returns relatively low for the effort expended. One can tire of chicken feathers and boiled shoelaces rather quickly when there's champagne and caviar for the asking right next door.

Then too, science fiction readers are a special case. They have no particular interest in art per se; their idea of a "pretty" picture is likely to be a bleak and barren moonscape or a closeup of the dunes of Mars; and if the factual detail in an artist's conception is not accurate to at least three decimals, their first impulse is to nail the artist's hide to the observatory door. On the other hand, when science fiction readers discover an artist who gives them covers which *do* illustrate the stories, while at the same time being technically good paintings as well as beautiful pictures, they clutch him to their collective bosom with an enthusiasm and affection which is one of the field's greatest rewards. (It even improves the flavor of shoelaces!)

They found such an artist at Big MAC—MidAmericon—The World Science Fiction Society's 34th annual convention, in Kansas City in 1976. That was the year Michael Whelan mounted a major display of his science fiction and fantasy cover paintings. It was not entirely coincidental that sales from the convention art show were the highest in science fiction history—the fans snapped up everything Michael had for sale and yelled for more. The publishers were only a step behind—in fact a couple of them were ahead by a length, and very shortly there was a Whelan cover everywhere you could look. And *good*! His recent treatment of Anne McCaffrey's dragons will provide an aiming-point (and a good deal of frustration!) to dragon-draughtsmen for years to come.

Michael doesn't consider himself to be exclusively an "sf and fantasy illustrator" (though it puts him in excellent company) but his paintings are so carefully thought out and lovingly executed as to fit every requirement of the very special disciplines of science fiction. Like all good illustrators Michael Whelan possesses a strong element of the showman, and the communicator; and he puts both abilities to work in every picture.

Brilliantly imaginative, intensely dedicated to the classic values of art qua art, a meticulous craftsman as concerned with the proper rendering of detail as with its relationship to the whole, he brings to every painting an imposing array of skills. Not the least of them is a constantly growing, searching, expanding vision which, in the end, is the very cornerstone of science fiction art.

I mentioned earlier that there are very few top-flight illustrators in the science fiction field at any given time....

Michael Whelan is one of them.

Kelly and Polly Freas
Virginia Beach, Virginia, 1978

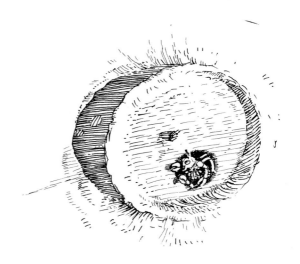

FOREWORD

A good artist is a good communicator. The art form may be written, oral, visual or a host of others, but the resulting creation must convey something to its audience. Therefore, the artist has to skillfully combine craftsmanship and approach so that an idea or feeling is clearly communicated to a significant number of people. In the field of illustration, this concept is complicated further by the illustrator's task of re-expressing the ideas of another artist: the author. Ultimately, not only must the artist communicate the thrust of someone else's ideas to a significant number of people, he also must do this in a manner consistent with the author's vision, while doing his best not to miscommunicate his own. Add to this the necessary element of commercialism and the illustrator's major dilemmas become apparent.

Successful communication in the field of editorial illustration involves two important considerations. First, like every good artist, the successful illustrator is a simplifier. His foremost talent is the ability to select and then to emphasize, subdue, or to omit given information in such a way that the message comes through. In other words, the fine editorial illustrator has a commitment to transcribe faithfully in visual form the most important aspects of a story. The task is made especially difficult by the demands of the field, because the second consideration facing the illustrator is that the image he creates must be salesworthy. Often, it has to survive poor color reproduction, clashing mammoth type, indiscriminate cropping, and generally unimaginative graphic design. In the special area of paperback book cover art (which represents the majority of my work to date) there are even more frustrating restrictions. For example, how can each cover illustration be unique and striking when the top third must be left "open" for title type and the whole image is to be reduced to a mere four by seven inches? The artist must walk a fine line between commercial necessities and aesthetic responsibilities. One wonders why such artwork should be bothered with at all! But for me, there's the irresistible challenge of creating a vital and expressive piece of art out of the inherent difficulties in commercial illustration.

And then there are the stories. I find a special attraction in fantasy and science fiction illustration: it's in the written material itself. There is a seemingly infinite variety of writing in this field and it calls for the greatest use of my imaginative and creative abilities. In doing fantasy and science fiction illustration, I can be absolutely faithful to a writer's story and still paint a picture that echoes fantasies I've nurtured since my first flight to Mars—aboard the spaceship I drew on the underside of my parents' coffee table when I was 4 years old. So, many of my own ideas and feelings go into my work. But because I strive to fulfill my obligation as an illustrator—to express narrative, characters, themes, or moods as the authors describe them—my paintings reflect a part of the author as well. Hence, the design of the book you are now holding. I've invited several authors for whose books I've done cover art to share with you some of their thoughts about the importance of good illustration. Together, my artwork and comments and the authors' views will tell you much about the field of science fiction and fantasy literature and its "packaging."

Here is *Wonderworks*—a look at the first years of my career as an editorial illustrator, but more importantly a communication of my own sense of wonder and my wish to inspire yours.

Michael Whelan
Brookfield, Conn.
Fall, 1978

SCIENCE FICTION

POUL ANDERSON

Far from being an insignificant offshoot of the "mainstream," fantasy is the well-spring of literature. It was likely the first form of storytelling, ages before the idea of writing existed. Certainly the oldest narratives we possess are fantasy, tales of gods and heroes who had adventures which could never happen in mundane life. Science fiction of a sort came along not much later; for example, the *Odyssey*. "Realistic" novels didn't appear until a mere thousand or so years ago, and have only become dominant in the past couple of centuries. Today we seem to be witnessing at least a modest resurgence in the popularity of the imaginative story.

Fantasy and science fiction art shares the same antiquity. Together with those splendid naturalistic cave paintings are works more enigmatic. From the earliest historic times onward, we get countless depictions of that on which no living eye ever fell. In our contemporary world, the literary revival of high-flying fancy has called forth an abundance of gifted artists to illustrate and enrich those dreams.

Over the years, I've seen covers and interior drawings for tales of mine, and learned for the most part to pay them scant heed, because the majority have been bad or mediocre. When a good one has come along, though, I have naturally been delighted. Well, I never had a greater experience of this kind than when I first saw simultaneously prints of Michael Whelan's cover paintings for novels by me that Ace Books was reprinting.

Why? The reason is twofold. First, he is an extremely fine artist by any standards. Composition, color, stances, facial expressions, all are marvelously handled, to produce scenes that are dramatic but

never melodramatic. Indeed, when for *The Night Face* an unconscious human is being carried off by a band of apelike creatures, the effect is precisely the half-mystical one for which the text strives; it's like a staging of *Ondine*. The eerie twilight on *World Without Stars*, the vigorous humor on *The Man Who Counts*, the sorrow on *Question and Answer*—these too show just what I was hoping to convey, which is most encouraging to me as a writer.

Thus we arrive at the second major reason for Whelan's importance. He *reads*. Remarkably few illustrators do, you know. Far too often (with honorable exceptions, of course) the pictures they produce bear little or no relationship to what the author was describing. Michael Whelan obviously studies manuscripts with care, then thinks hard, before starting work. I assure you that in everything mentioned above, and surely in most everything else, he has gotten settings and people—including nonhuman people—exactly right.

Therefore, long though the history of imaginative art is and brilliant though many of its practitioners have been, already he has made his own considerable mark upon it. I suspect that soon he will undertake things still more ambitious, and I look forward to that, even if it may cost us his services in regular fantasy and science fiction. What couldn't he do with, say, the old mythologies, Shakespeare, or the Bible? Meanwhile, and in any event, let us rejoice that he is among us.

Poul Anderson

THE NIGHT FACE

An occasion on which I used a model. I took a Polaroid shot of myself lying on the floor to help me get the foreshortening correct on this one. The result was ghastly: it looked like a grimy police morgue photo—with me as the victim!

Acrylics on Illustration Board
Cover painting for the book by Poul Anderson, published by
Ace Books, Inc., New York, New York. Copyright © 1977 by Michael R. Whelan.

Color Sketch

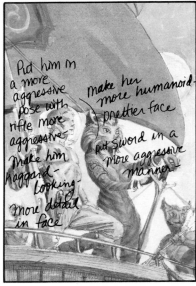

...With Art Director's Comments

Full-size Pencil Drawing

Painting in Progress

ENSIGN FLANDRY

Acrylics on Illustration Board

Cover painting for the book by Poul Anderson,
published by Ace Books, Inc., New York, New York.
Copyright © 1979 by Michael R. Whelan.

THE MAN WHO COUNTS

Nicholas Van Rijn, the ultimate diplomat, cons the reluctant Dromedian aliens into carrying him over their ocean. As you can see, this was no small task—it took three of them to carry the hefty hero.

Acrylics on Masonite

Cover painting for the book by Poul Anderson, published by Ace Books, Inc., New York, New York. Copyright © 1977 by Michael R. Whelan.

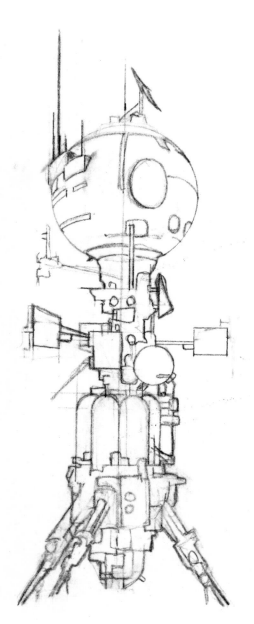

ARMAGEDDON

Even after all humankind has been wiped out, mechanized engines of destruction continue to eradicate the last traces of civilization.

Acrylics on Illustration Board
Painting done for a
gallery show on the theme
"Machines on Wheels."
Copyright © 1976 by
Michael R. Whelan.
First publication.

Unused cover sketch

TIME AND AGAIN

A great story, too complex to represent faithfully in a single narrative illustration. Instead, a
scene created to contain several key elements
from the plot (the glowing eyes, torn spacesuit,
book, envelope, broken window), in order to
focus on the *mood* of the story and pique the
interest of the potential reader.

Acrylics on Illustration Board
Cover painting for the book by Clifford D.
Simak, published and copyright © 1976 by Ace
Books, Inc., New York, New York. Reprinted
by permission.

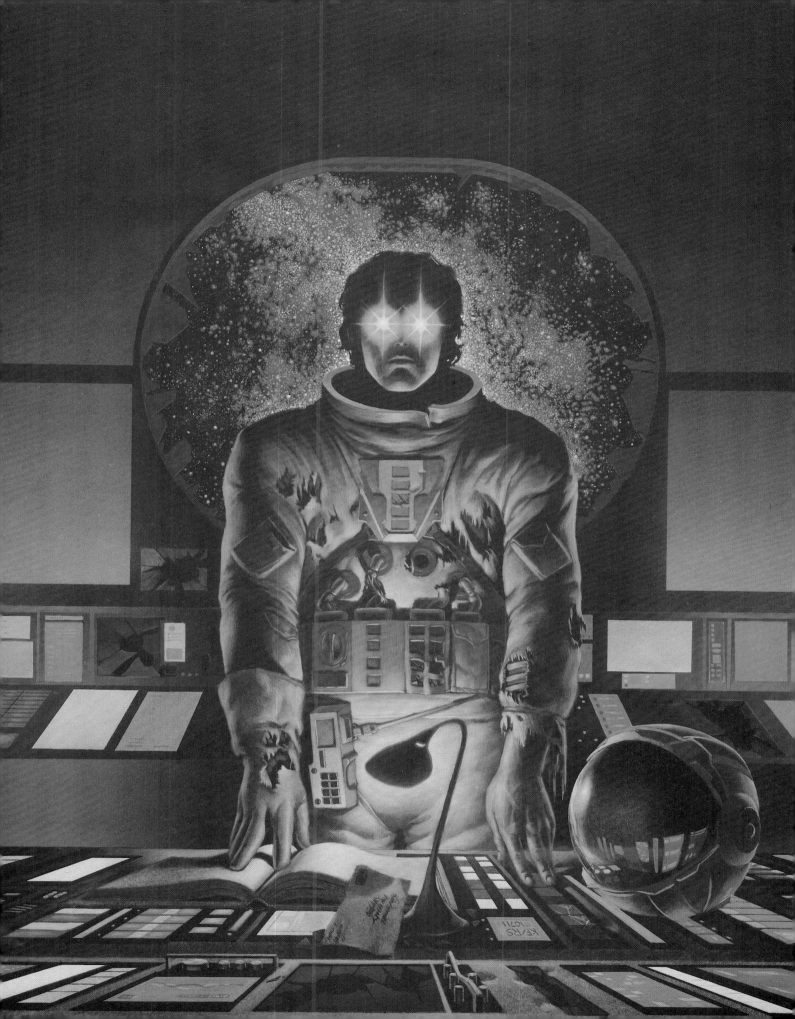

THE BLOODY SUN

My first cover assignment for Ace Books.

Acrylics on Illustration Board

THE TROUBLE WITH TYCHO

While excavating on the Moon, an astronaut bites the dust (I couldn't resist) and the other fights vainly against a malevolent alien energy. For the first time in my professional career, I incorporated my signature into the design of an object in the illustration—the living astronaut's patch.

Acrylics on Illustration Board

Cover painting for the book by Clifford D. Simak, published and Copyright © 1976 by Ace Books, Inc., New York, New York. In the collection of Mr. Larry Vaught. Reprinted by permission.

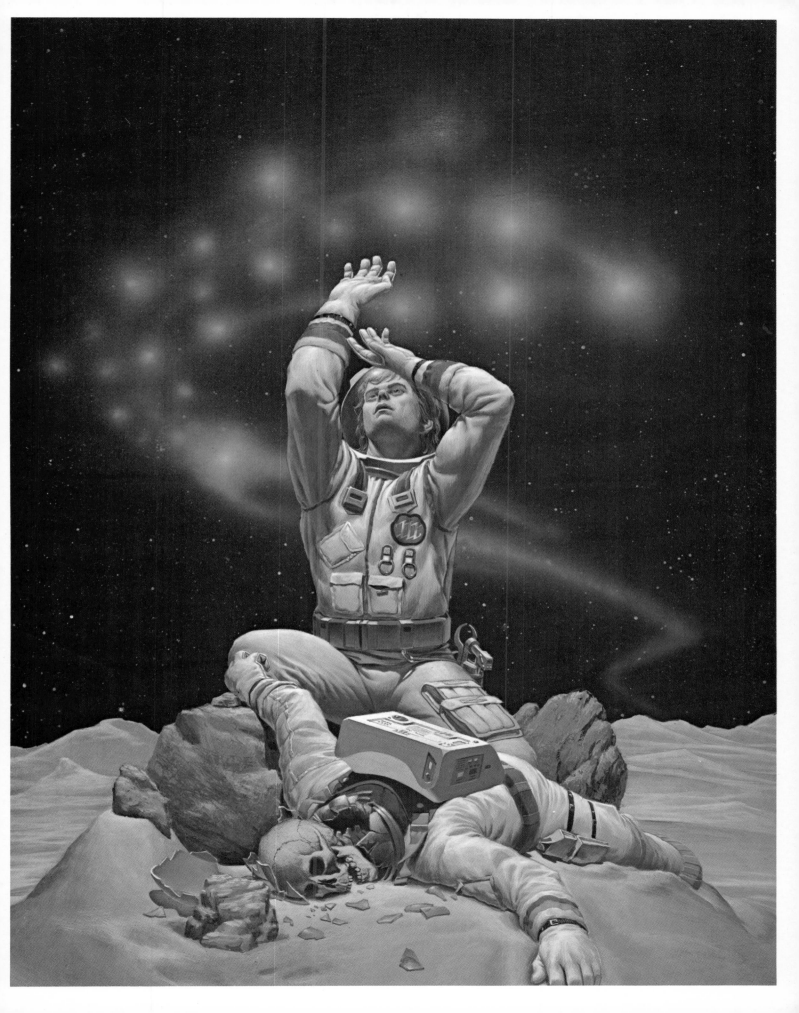

A STUDY OF BOWIE

During the summer of 1976, I heard that in an upcoming issue, *Time* magazine was going to do a cover story on science fiction. I took a week out of my regular schedule to do this sample cover idea. *Time* never did the story, but it gave me a good chance to try my hand at this type of cover assignment.

Acrylics on Illustration Board

Color sketch selected by Art Director for cover.

BROTHER ASSASSIN

I am often kidded about my general dislike for yellow; but sometimes it insists on dominating a color scheme and to make matters worse—it works!

Acrylics on Illustration Board

Cover painting for the book by Fred Saberhagen, published by Ace Books, Inc., New York, New York. Copyright © 1978 by Michael R. Whelan.

Unused cover sketch

CITY

An airbrush can be a great time-saving tool in rendering backgrounds, but sometimes I enjoy knowing that even if the power went off I could still produce a smooth gradation of color over a large area. On this painting I used conventional brushes. Three boards and thirty-two washes later I had exactly the blue I wanted!

Acrylics on Illustration Board

Cover painting for the book by Clifford D. Simak, published and copyright © 1976 by Ace Books, Inc., New York, New York. Reprinted by permission.

SWORD & SORCERY

MICHAEL MOORCOCK

Michael Whelan is perhaps the best artist regularly to illustrate my American paperback editions. He seems to be able to cater for the genre demands whilst giving a decent interpretation of the characters and moods of the books. This is particularly true of *Elric*. The market demands muscles (my hero is actually something of a weakling), so Whelan has done muscles. But, he has brought up the demonic element in the character—his griefs, his internal struggles and so on—and has emphasized the sword, the alien qualities of my protagonist, and the wild, romantic landscapes. This is evident in what I think is his best cover in the series (although they are all far better than most I get)—the cover for *Stormbringer!* This is probably the best book in the series and my own particular favourite and Whelan appears to have pulled out all stops on depicting Elric at the height of his struggle—internal, external, and cosmic!

Having suffered from some pretty extraordinary Elrics (several on early paperbacks and magazine covers were unrecognizable—one was black, doubtless because the artist had looked up albinoism in the dictionary and found it sometimes referred to "white negroes" in an area of Africa once controlled by the Portuguese!); and so I am more than usually grateful for an artist who not only depicts him as I imagine (and describe him), but who also manages to capture some of the appropriate atmosphere; for in a romance of this sort hero and landscape are essentially one thing.

Moreover it's a pleasure to have an artist who can draw. Too often a decent cover idea has been marred by the simple fact that the artist in question isn't very good at simple anatomical detail. Fantasy subject matter is often an excuse to obscure and tangle-over mistakes which would never be allowed in other types of paintings. It's something from which Whelan's work is by and large refreshingly free. Fantasy art, like fantasy fiction, demands certain disciplines which must be firmly adhered to if the work is going to be worthwhile. These days there are too many bad artists drawing monsters and "alien" people, because their draughtsmanship and sense of anatomy isn't all it should be. You never get this feeling with Whelan. You feel he could do a perfectly straightforward painting if he chose to. His work has that kind of authority which the best sword and sorcery has. You know the authors could write pretty much anything they cared to—but what they enjoyed doing was fantasy. Michael Whelan obviously enjoys doing fantasy too and as a result I have a series of covers far better than any series of covers I have had in America before.

Michael Whelan

STORMBRINGER

I remember trying to get in the mood of painting for the last time the albino sorcerer king, Elric. I took a clothes rail out of a closet for my sword and ran around outside slashing at weeds and lunging at the breeze. I began to feel quite majestic and imagined myself atop the ruins of the end of the world. When I slipped into the pose that captured the feeling of the whole story, I knew that this sense of "freezing of action" was too important to lose; so, instead of setting up the pose for my camera and possibly losing its freshness, I rushed into my studio and drew it from memory.

Acrylics on Masonite

Cover painting for the book by Michael Moorcock, published by DAW Books, Inc., New York, New York.

Frontispiece for *The Enchantress of World's End*

THE ENCHANTRESS OF
WORLD'S END

My first paperback cover assignment.

Mixed Media on Illustration Board

Cover painting for the book by Lin Carter,
published and copyright © 1975 by DAW Books, Inc.,
New York, New York. In the collection of
Mr. Lin Carter. Reprinted by permission.

THE RENEGADE OF KREGEN

Acrylics on Illustration Board

Cover painting for the book by Alan Burt
Akers. Published by DAW Books, Inc.,
New York, New York. Copyright © 1976 by
Michael R. Whelan. In the collection of
Mr. and Mrs. Walter W. Larsen.

THE KING OF THE DEAD

Gouache on Illustration Board

Cover painting for *The Bane of the Black Sword* by Michael Moorcock, published by DAW Books, Inc., New York, New York. Copyright © 1977 by Michael R. Whelan. In the collection of Mr. and Mrs. Randal Hawkins.

URISH'S BANE

A fascinating book that gave me the fun of painting a "no-holds-barred" demon. In many ways I did this one for *me*—dark—and I'm pleased it has received such a positive response from the readers.

Acrylics on Masonite

Cover painting for *The Vanishing Tower* by Michael Moorcock, published by DAW Books, Inc., New York, New York. Copyright © 1976 by Michael R. Whelan.

THE WHITE WOLF

Elric derives his strength and magical powers from his sword *Stormbringer* which feeds on the souls of those it kills.

Oils and Acrylics on Illustration Board
Cover painting for *The Weird of the White Wolf*
by Michael Moorcock, published by DAW Books, Inc.,
New York, New York. Copyright © 1977 by Michael R.
Whelan. In the collection of Mr. and Mrs.
Randal Hawkins.

SWORDS AND ICE MAGIC

Although there are many wonderful scenes in this story and the others in the series, the most important aspect of these works to me is the characterization of the heroes, Fafhrd and the Grey Mouser. My primary concern, then, was to portray them as accurately as possible. To my knowledge this had not been done before on a book cover.

Acrylics on Illustration Board

Cover painting for the book by Fritz Leiber,
published by Ace Books, Inc., New York, New York.
Copyright © 1977 by Michael R. Whelan.

SAILOR ON THE SEAS OF FATE

Nice things sometimes come out of necessity. My usual dilemma—keeping the top third of the painting empty enough for type—was solved by the misty fog that envelopes the scene. The usual riggings, sail, and mast are somewhat obscured and fade away behind it, leaving plenty of room for the type and setting —exactly the mood that the author created to surround his mystical anti-hero, Elric.

Acrylics on Illustration Board

Cover painting for the book by Michael Moorcock, published by DAW Books, Inc., New York, New York. Copyright © 1976 by Michael R. Whelan. In the collection of Mr. George Barr.

ROMANTIC FANTASY

ANNE MCCAFFREY

When Judy-Lynn del Rey of Del Rey Books told me that she had commissioned Michael Whelan to do the covers of the new editions of the Dragonrider of Pern books, I had the temerity (all for the love of dragons) to write him what my dragons *aren't* (like scaled, fanged, eared and snake-long in the neck). In spite of my nervous interference, Michael Whelan has produced magnificent illustrations of what my dragons *are!*

I was relieved to see Lessa, for once, appropriately clad for dragonriding on the cover of *Dragonflight*. Equally appropriate is the mood, Lessa leading the dragons of the Weyr, all gold above a shadowy green world.

Obviously, Michael read all three books!

I remember how often John Campbell exhorted me to put the Pern dragons in combat, searing Thread from the skies. So Michael's concept on the cover of *Dragonquest* especially delights me.

But *The White Dragon* is *the* cover! For starters, it stands out like a lure in any bookshop window, that proud white dragon with his handsome young rider. Just examine that cover closely and see how much Michael Whelan has managed to illustrate. He has subtly touched on the ambivalence of the hero's position, hinted at his strength of character, clearly depicted the dragon's beauty and size, added the darting curiosity of the fire-lizards haunting dragon and rider, the rough, harsh landscape of the beleaguered planet Pern, and the significantly distant figures of dragonriders silhouetted against the dreaded Red Star.

Fortunate indeed is the author who has Michael Whelan for illustrator.

Anne McCaffrey

55

THE WHITE DRAGON

Even with Ms. McCaffrey's rather specific description of her dragons of Pern, I found plenty of room for individual interpretation. The preliminary drawings reproduced here show the evolution of my concept of the fantastic winged beasts.

Acrylics on Masonite

Cover painting for the book by Anne McCaffrey, published by Ballantine/Del Rey Books, New York, New York. Copyright © 1978 by Michael R. Whelan.

DRAGONFLIGHT (overleaf)

Acrylics on Masonite

Cover painting for the book by Anne McCaffrey,
published by Ballantine/Del Rey Books, New York,
New York. Copyright © 1978 by Michael R. Whelan.
In the collection of Mr. Lex Nakashima.

ALEX

One of the few paperback covers I've done in which the only reference made to the inside material is that of a mysterious mood. When exhibited, this painting always seems to be overshadowed by other pieces of my work, but it remains one of my personal favorites.

Acrylics on Illustration Board

Cover painting for *Dying For Tomorrow* by Michael Moorcock, published by DAW Books, Inc., New York, New York. Copyright © 1977 by Michael R. Whelan.

AT EIRLU

First of an uncompleted series of paintings on the theme of Astral Projection. Though I did this one in early 1974, I still hope to do the other two someday; the images remain clear in my mind, waiting to be put down on paper.

Water Colors on Water Color Paper

A SPELL FOR CHAMELEON

Though he would as soon eat you as talk to you, a manticore can be an excellent conversationalist.

Acrylics on Illustration Board

Cover painting for the book by Piers Anthony, published by Ballantine/Del Rey Books, New York, New York. Copyright © 1977 by Michael R. Whelan.

LORD KALVAN OF OTHERWHEN

Occasionally I'm called upon to come up with a cover painting for a science fiction book that doesn't have any of the conventional symbols for SF recognized by the general public (i.e. planets, stars, spaceships, futuristic cities, etc.). In this case I utilized the juxtaposition of the barbaric surroundings with the pistol in Kalvan's hand—a distinctly modern device.

Acrylics on Masonite
Cover painting for the book by H. Beam Piper,
published by Ace Books, Inc., New York, New York.
Copyright © 1976 by Michael R. Whelan.

HORROR

GERALD W. PAGE

One of the major problems in publishing fantasy has been illustration, particularly cover illustration. When the science fiction magazines came along, artists like Frank R. Paul were able to find elements to include in their paintings and drawings that exactly pinpointed what SF was all about: Paul's painting for the first issue of *Amazing* might be one of the most crudely painted covers he ever did, but it could not be mistaken for anything but science fiction with that gigantic image of Saturn right above the heads of those ice skaters.

It was the work Paul did for the first issues of *Amazing* that set the pace for the style.

Fantasy presented greater problems. You can identify a scene as science fiction by featuring a spaceship, for example, but the elements that make a story fantasy are more subtle. Horror is a phase of fantasy that seems to present the artist with even greater problems than other types. For starters, it's just as hard to isolate an identifiable element for the cover of a book of horror stories as it is for any book of straight fantasies. But other problems enter in. Problem One is taste. It's very easy for the element of horror to give way to one of sadism, an element that usually has very little to do with horror. The second problem is originality. When I want an illustration for a good vampire story, nothing makes me angrier than to have an artist give me a drawing of Bela Lugosi. Movie monsters belong in the movies. Artists who base their concepts of horror illustration on movies aren't using their imaginations.

An artist who *does* use his imagination is Michael Whelan. The first three volumes in DAW Books' series *The Year's Best Horror Stories* were edited by Richard Davis. I started with number four. It was the first effort of mine to have a Whelan illustration. He gave us a nice serene blue cover with an almost surrealistic gathering of traditional horror elements such as the spider, that demon in the window, a lizard monster, bats—lots of bats—and something wormy thawing out nicely on that fellow's shoulder. Traditional elements, yes, but hardly a traditional arrangement.

For Series V, Michael Whelan went from peaceful blue to a bright and almost cheerful orange. And appropriate it is, because what looks more cheerful than the inescapable grin of a skull? Especially as demonstrated here by one of Michael's favorite models. Whelan's incredible eye for detail is shown once again, in such touches as the bracelet on our subject's wrist, and the bookmark protruding from the pages of his journal. And don't overlook the intricate design on the back of that chair.

The trick in doing a series—writing one, editing it, or doing the illustrations—is to come up with something each outing that's better than what you did previously. It's not easy. Year after year, few people can manage it. Whelan always seems to come up with something for *The Year's Best Horror Stories* that tops what's gone before. Once again, his relish for this type of work is very evident, as is the relish of the subject for whatever work it is he's about. In fact, this is a first-rate character painting—though I wouldn't want to meet this character—especially in isolated circumstances! Again, note the detailing, but pay special attention to the professionalism with which that detailing is displayed. This is a very simple, direct painting, and the details were carefully selected for effect, and used sparingly so that they don't overwhelm the painting. Good taste, you see, applies not only to subject, but also to every facet of a painting, and how these facets are presented.

Since I became the editor of *The Year's Best Horror Stories* series, I've been very lucky in having covers by Michael Whelan. His work has been eye-catching, product-identifying, tasteful, and original. His highly developed technique, his color sense, and especially his attention to detail conjure a spell that must have accounted for a lot of bookstand sales.

Gerald W Page

BLUE FEAR

The cover of *The Year's Best Horror Stories* is a job I always look forward to doing. It is usually the only time during the year that I paint a picture not related to a specific written work and it gives me a chance to put down wholly self-derived concepts. I am still illustrating, but I've shifted the focus to communicating the mood rather than the narrative.

Acrylics on Illustration Board

Cover painting for *The Year's Best Horror
Stories—Series IV*, edited by Gerald W. Page,
published and copyright © 1976 by DAW Books, Inc.,
New York, New York. Reprinted by permission.

THE PEEPER

When I first moved to the East Coast in search of illustration jobs, I had to prepare a portfolio with a selection of the variety of work I was able to do. This was the "horror" piece that I took around to the art directors.

Oils on Illustration Board

NIGHT-GAUNTS

Out of what crypt they crawl, I cannot tell,
But every night I see the rubbery things,
Black, horned, and slender, with membra-
    nous wings,
They come in legions on the north wind's swell
With obscene clutch that titillates and stings,
Snatching me off on monstrous voyagings
To grey worlds hidden deep in nightmare's
    well.

Over the jagged peaks of Thok they sweep,
Heedless of all the cries I try to make,
And down the nether pits to that foul lake
Where the puffed shoggoths splash in doubt-
    ful sleep.
But ho! If only they would make some sound,
Or wear a face where faces should be found!

from *Fungi From Yuggoth & Other Poems*
by H. P. Lovecraft

EREBUS

I was beginning to feel that I had pigeonholed myself with this series into three-dimensional variations of montages. I needed a change. This was originally done very small, in pen and ink, for a bookplate design and I couldn't resist developing it into a full color painting.

Acrylics on Illustration Board

Cover painting for *The Year's Best Horror Stories—Series V*, edited by Gerald W. Page, published by DAW Books, Inc., New York, New York. Copyright © 1977 by Michael R. Whelan.

SMILER

Horror makes its most profound impact in otherwise prosaic situations, though I am sure there are horrific things aplenty on the streets of any city at night.

Acrylics on Masonite

Cover painting for *The Year's Best Horror Stories—Series VI*, edited by Gerald W. Page, published by DAW Books, Inc., New York, New York. Copyright © 1978 by Michael R. Whelan.

Unused cover sketch

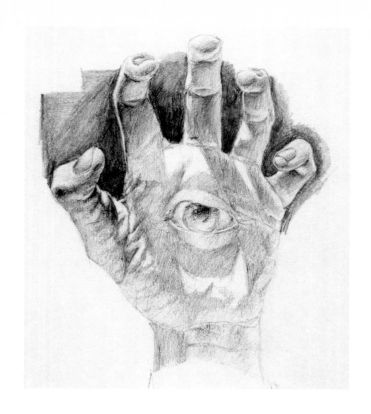

VISIONS OF CASSANDRA

The central images came to me when I was still in college. Five years later when I received the cover assignment, they resurfaced and I committed them to canvas. An example of how a commercial assignment can still satisfy one's creative impulses.

Acrylics on Canvas Board

Cover painting for *The Year's Best Horror Stories—Series III*, edited by Richard Davis, published and copyright © 1975 by DAW Books, Inc., New York, New York. Owner unknown. Reprinted by permission.

HEROINES

C. J. CHERRYH

To my mind, there cannot be so great a difference between the imagination of the writer and that of the artist. Both *see*. A writer's instinct is to tell that vision in such elaboration and detail that the reader can live through that moment and into others, a flowing process and internal. An artist captures that same vision in an instant, wholly—freezes all the individual moments of it into the attitude of a body, the set of a hand, a face, the quality of the light: one moment which implies and evokes all the others.

That, to me, is illustration. It's a joy as a writer to open that thin envelope from my publisher and to unveil a cover proof like the one for *Gate of Ivrel*—to see, suddenly, the same vision which I lived during the months of my solitary work now made visible. I look at it as into a mirror of my own mind, *seeing*, for the first time the thoughts of someone else casting back my own: *my* people reflected through other eyes and now become someone else's too. The moment brings a curious

sense of affirmation—a feeling that, unlike daydreams that vanish, now they are real: someone else has seen the vision too, and others will see it after.

Aha, I say, I know these people. That's the way they were when I last saw them.

And I know that in partnership with and regardless of all the words I have laid down in the book—that will be the vision of all the readers who come to it. My people will look so to them; most readers will hardly be aware whether they obtained their vision from the cover or from my words: indeed, likely both are inextricably intertwined. That is the power of illustration. I have been asked questions at times about a character's nature or origin or attitude, and the questioner adds: "They *looked* as if..."—without seeming to be aware that there are two sources for his impression. It's that partnership of words and art invoked again.

It is a great joy when both agree so well...when that recognition strikes me, down to the smallest degrees of habit. I build worlds as well as events. The illustration opens the door and lets me see what I've done: there's Mount Ivrel; there's the crumbling keep of Ohtij-in—and now I know that the reader will see them in a certain way. There is sometimes, as a writer, yet another point of recognition... for often when I conceive a story there are places in it so intensely visual, which strike my mind with such force, that I write toward these moments and away from them as if they were landmarks on a map...and to see, on unveiling that cover proof, that one of those moments *is* the cover—gives a strange sense that minds have somehow been in touch.

Surely fantasy and science fiction require that peculiar sharing of vision: both work upon mood and feeling, and to capture the wonder of alien worlds and the fragile essence of magic—in range of the eye—takes a very special skill. And to transfer that capture to touches of color and fix it forever, visible to my eyes and others'—that is purely wizardly.

C. J. Cherryh

GATE OF IVREL

Acrylics and oils on Canvas Board

Cover for the book by C. J. Cherryh, published
and copyright © 1975 by DAW Books, Inc., New York,
New York. In the collection of Ron Miller.
Reprinted by permission.

b/w sketch

Painting in progress

WELL OF SHIUAN

One of the most intriguing aspects of the character Morgaine is her spell-sword, *Changeling.* As described in the story, it rips apart the very fabric of time and space to send her enemies wheeling off into a dark and nameless void. (Which all sounds great, but is tough to realize visually.)

Acrylics on Masonite

Cover painting for the book by C. J. Cherryh, published by DAW Books, Inc., New York, New York. Copyright © 1977 by Michael R. Whelan.

EARTHCHILD

Earthchild is a fascinating story; for sheer un-bridled imagination it has few peers. My cover painting is a somewhat symbolic representation of the three main characters: Reee, the last person left on Earth, Emeroo (in the shape of the egg), her foster mother, and Indigo, the intelligent blue protoplasm intent upon assimilating the entire planet...Reee and Emeroo included!

Acrylics on Masonite

Cover painting for the book by Doris Piserchia, published by DAW Books, Inc., New York, New York.
Copyright © 1977 by Michael R. Whelan.

DIADEM FROM THE STARS

Acrylics on Canvas Board

Cover painting for the book by Jo Clayton,
published by DAW Books, Inc., New York, New York.
Copyright © 1976 by Michael R. Whelan.

LAMARCHOS

As described in the book, the skies of the planet Lamarchos are alive with floating aerobic bacteria of every conceivable hue, which paint the atmosphere in swirling, ever changing clouds of color. In this foreign and surreal environment, our heroine Aleytys—clad like the natives only in body paint and hair dye—uses her amplified mental powers to topple an enemy spacecraft.

Acrylics on Illustration Board

Cover painting for the book by Jo Clayton,
published by DAW Books, Inc., New York, New York.
Copyright © 1977 by Michael R. Whelan. In the
collection of Sid Altus.

THE GAMEPLAYERS OF ZAN

An unusual side of this cover was that the author told Donald Wolheim what scene should appear on the cover. My task, then, was to paint "a mental image of a woman revolving in blue boxes over an infinite control panel with a star pattern all around her." (!)

Acrylics on Masonite
Cover painting for the book by M. A. Foster,
published by DAW Books, Inc., New York, New York.
Copyright © 1976 by Michael R. Whelan.

AUDREY ON ZARATHUSTRA (overleaf)

Someone once said, "There are but two boons in life: the love of art and the art of love." What a pleasure to combine the two!

Acrylics on Masonite

Illustration for **Under The Green Star's Spell** by Lin Carter, published and copyright© 1976 by DAW Books, Inc., New York, New York.

ALIENS

ALAN DEAN FOSTER

A roundball metaphor: Michael Whelan is the Bill Walton of science fiction art.

Whelan does his work with brush and pen, Walton with a basketball, yet both are artists. The former applies his talents to canvas, the latter to a metal hoop of modest diameter.

Neither is the most spectacular performer in his chosen field. There are others flashier, glitter-spangled and noisy in their accomplishments who elicit occasional louder yelps from their respective audiences. Art has its own hotdogs. But there are none who do their job as competently and with such seeming naturalness and ease as these two. The cheers they receive may not always be as loud, but they are delivered with truer feelings, and more often.

In Michael Whelan this astonishing ease and versatility shows as a kind of subdued confidence of composition, the mark of the master illustrator. Looking at any Whelan painting you always have the feeling that it could have been more electric, more blatant, more obvious, but that the artist was concerned first with doing his job, illustrating. There are paintings of his that could be more muscular, but Michael eschews special effects for their own sake. His heroes are never ninety-pound weaklings, but unlike the particular work of the Arnold Schwarzenegger school of anatomy, Michael's people look natural, look real, look like they have powerful bodies which might actually seem normal on a real human being. A Whelan painting is many things, but never meretricious.

Besides this quiet confidence, there is the still untapped versatility of which Whelan is capable. Notice, as you flip through these pages, the things that Michael paints that most artists don't or can't paint. The little items of everyday otherworldy life. Pull yourself away from

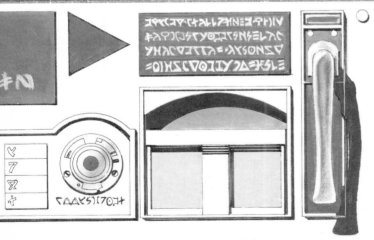

painting an incomplete piece. I believe he'd put them in to satisfy himself no matter the commercial requirements. His visions are lifted whole and intact from other dimensions, and he desires us fortunate ones to share in the completeness of those visions.

I must not forget the light. The utilization of light is the ultimate spice of the painter, often subtle but vitally important, like the saffron in a good paella. Michael is a subtle worker, dealing in mysterious shadows and ghost images, suggesting and hinting, making the viewer work for his aesthetic reward.

Take a look at the cover he did for my own collection of stories, *With Friends Like These*. Study first the self-portrait of Audrey and Michael (hint: they are not the ones on the sidelines). Now smile at the perplexed, bemused, yet accurately rendered aliens. Pass beyond the sly smile of the central figure, the artist to whom this tome does homage.

What do we discover? It is the source of light for this particular composition, there and yet not there, hinted at and yet definitely included. A five-paned window.

That's the signatory, the hallmark of Michael Whelan the artist, for he paints the not-there as well as the more obvious, and makes you hunt for it and squeal with delight at the finding. He draws our eyes back for a second time, and a third, and such multiple curtain calls of the eye are the finest compliment that can be paid to any concretizer of the impossible. . . .

the dynamic poses and flaming swords to take a minute and examine the furniture, the masonry, the weapons and clothing and plants in these wonderfully workable compositions. They're not there because they're vital to the illustration, but because I don't think Michael Whelan is capable of

WITH FRIENDS LIKE THESE

Audrey and I are "ice cream addicts" so we were naturals for the roles of the farmer and his wife who entertain a small group of alien ambassadors in their country kitchen. This was the only time I deliberately used either one of us in a cover painting.

Acrylics on Illustration Board

Cover painting for the book by Alan Dean Foster, published by Ballantine/Del Rey Books, New York, New York. Copyright © 1977 by Michael R. Whelan.

VALLAND'S SONG

Probably too dark to be an effective paper-back cover; nevertheless it's a favorite of mine. I plead intense emotional involvement in the story as my excuse for perhaps overlooking the difficulty in reproducing it for commercial use.

Acrylics on Illustration Board

Cover painting for *World Without Stars* by Poul Anderson, published by Ace Books, Inc., New York, New York. Copyright © 1977 by Michael R. Whelan.

LITTLE FUZZY

No, this is not my bid for the title of "the Charles Keene of Science Fiction." But how else could I portray furry little aliens who are described as being "irresistibly cute"? I've never met nor seen a picture of H. Beam Piper, but I've been told that the way I depicted the hero Pappy Jack bears some resemblance to him.

Acrylics on Illustration Board

Cover painting for the book by H. Beam Piper, published and copyright © 1975 by Ace Books, Inc., New York, New York. In the collection of Mr. and Mrs. Walter M. Larsen. Reprinted by permission.

FUZZY SAPIENS (overleaf)

Charles Volpe, the art director at Ace Books, couldn't choose between two of my color sketches for this job; so, he asked me to combine them on one wraparound cover.

Acrylics on Illustration Board

Cover painting for the book by H. Beam Piper, published and copyright © 1976 by Ace Books, Inc., New York, New York. In the collection of Mr. Martin T. Price. Reprinted by permission.

RUN FOR COVER

Acrylics on Illustration Board

Cover painting for *The Fuzzy Papers*, published by
Doubleday Books, Inc. Copyright © 1976 by Michael
R. Whelan.

QUESTION AND ANSWER

Acrylics on Masonite

Cover painting for the book by Poul Anderson,
published by Ace Books, Inc., New York, New York.
Copyright © 1977 by Michael R. Whelan.

THE PLANET SAVERS

As per the art director's instructions, I finally had the chance to design a cover with space for the type in the middle. I finished it leaving a light area in the center left and delivered it, only to find that the art director had changed his mind and wanted the type on top. Home again, I added pieces of board to the top and sides, filled in the cracks with modeling paste, and managed to match the paint and enlarge it so that there was plenty of room for the type on top. It was a struggle, but when I left my studio to go have lunch, I was pleased with how the painting had turned out. But when I returned, my studio was in a shambles. While I was gone my cat had tried to climb up my drawing board. She must have slipped on the smooth surface of the painting and tried to grasp it with her claws, because there were scratch marks all down the front. I was able to fix it and the painting still hangs in my living room as a testimonial to my patience...well, stubbornness, at least!

Acrylics on Illustration Board

Cover painting for the book by Marion Zimmer Bradley, published and copyright © 1976 by Ace Books, Inc., New York, New York. Reprinted by permission.

BIOGRAPHICAL OUTLINE

1950 Michael Whelan was born June 29, in Culver City, California, to Nancy and William R. Whelan. His father is an aerospace engineer, so most of Michael's childhood was spent moving frequently to various parts of California and Colorado. He has two sisters, Lorie and Wendy.

1955 This was the year of Michael's first big adventure. He ran away from home, but the police caught up with him at the nearest supermarket. After they took him home, still angry, he went into the garage, found some nails and plywood, and began building a "spaceship." "What are you doing?" his mother asked. Michael replied, "I'm going to Mars!"

1965-66 Whelan attended summer classes at Rocky Mountain School of Art in Denver, Colorado.

1968 He graduated from Oak Grove High School, San Jose, California and entered San Jose State University to study Art and the Biological Sciences. Whelan financed his education by working as a gas station attendant, managing a health food store, and was a convalescent home orderly. Later, he became an aide in the college's Anatomy/ Physiology Lab, built anatomical models, and illustrated for the *Journal of Bone and Joint Surgery*. Under the tutelage of M.D. Stewart and Dr. R.F. Brose, Whelan was encouraged to concentrate on Art as his major and it was then that his plans for a career as an illustrator began.

1973 Michael graduated as a President's Scholar and received his Bachelor's Degree with Great Distinction.

1974 January found Whelan enrolled at The Art Center College of Design in Los Angeles. After only nine months, his instructors felt that he was ready for his first commercial assignment. Michael left the college and was commissioned for his first paperback cover job by Donald Wollheim of DAW Books in New York.

1975 From January until March, Michael Whelan worked for DAW and Marvel Comics and received his first paperback cover assignment from Ace Books.

1976 He continued to work primarily for DAW and Ace and exhibited his paintings at the Green Grass Gallery, New York, New York and Norman Kramer Gallery, Danbury, Connecticut.

1977 Whelan was hired to do his first paperback cover for Ballantine/Del Rey Books in March. Later that year, he did the covers for the popular *Dragonflight* series by Anne McCaffrey, including the hardcover dustjacket for *The White Dragon*.

1978 By the end of this year, the artist had completed his ninetieth paperback cover and a cover and feature article in *Isaac Asimov's Science Fiction Magazine*.

Michael Whelan has been nominated as best professional artist for the Hugo (World Science Fiction) Award and for the Howard (World Fantasy) Award and he has exhibited and won prizes at numerous science fiction and fantasy conventions. He has recently completed for Ballantine/Del Rey Books the prestigious *John Carter of Mars* series by Edgar Rice Burroughs.